CLAIMING THE BIG BAD Wolf

Olive Spencer

Copyright © 2024 Olive Spencer

All rights reserved. This book or any portion thereof may not be reproduced or used in any manner whatsoever without the express written permission of the publisher except for the use of brief quotations in a book review.

First printing, 2024.

Ruthless Publishing
807 Holmes Drive, Studio LR
Colorado Springs, CO, 80909

www.olivespencer.com
www.library.olivespencer.com

Also by Olive Spencer

Contemporary Erotica
Sealed With A Kiss
Playing By The Rules

Contemporary Erotica
More than Words
A Dolly for Christmas
A Valentine for Dolly

Paranormal Erotica
Blood Lust
Blood Lust Crimson Temptations
Blood Lust Eternal Hunger (The Collection)
Ghosted

Erotic Romance
Working for the Big Bad Wolf
Taming the Big Bad Wolf
Old Enough to Know Better

Freebies:
Plaything – Working for the Big Bad Wolf
Playing Telephone – Working for the Big Bad Wolf
Blow Me, Harkness – Ghosted
Feeding Frenzy – Blood Lust

library.olivespencer.com

Dedication

For the girls who wanted a billionaire sugar daddy and ended up with a working class glucose guardian, this is for you.
And also for Eliza.

Content Warning

This book contains sex between two consenting adults. While Mina may call Grant her 'uncle' there is no blood relation between them.

Contents

Prologue	*1*
Chapter One	*2*
Chapter Two	*7*
Chapter Three	*11*
Chapter Four	*16*
Chapter Five	*19*
Chapter Six	*24*
Chapter Seven	*29*
Chapter Eight	*33*
Chapter Nine	*38*
Chapter Ten	*43*
Chapter Eleven	*46*
Chapter Twelve	*50*
Chapter Thirteen	*54*
Chapter Fourteen	*59*
Epilogue	*63*

Acknowledgements
About the Author
Where to find Olive Online
Thank You

Prologue

Fucking my best friend's daughter was my first mistake. Falling in love with her was another. My third and final mistake? Letting her walk out of my life without getting to say goodbye. That's the mistake I can't live with.

When I'm given the chance to reconcile with my princess, I don't take it lightly. I rush through a rainstorm to be by her side. When I learn that she took a part of me with her when she left, all I can do is stay.

I'm never leaving her again.

I'm never letting her walk out of my life.

Mina is my everything, my only thing, and now that we're bringing a child into the world?

I'm going to give her everything she's ever wanted. Everything she deserves.

It's time for the fairytale to have the happily-ever-after ending it deserves.

I want my best friend's daughter and our baby, and I always get what I want.

Chapter One

I arrive at Mina's apartment with my heart in my throat and a pit in my stomach. My heart beats like a drum solo, and I feel dizzy. The drive to Connecticut was long and dreary, giving me time to think about the predicament we find ourselves in. I replay her words over and over, her voice echoing in my brain like the refrain of a sad song.

"Come get me, Uncle Grant."

I've done the math over and over in my head, counting back the days. The last week of July, we were in heaven. Mina loved me, I loved her, and we did everything to consummate that love. One slip-up, one mistake, and it cost me everything. My life, my happiness, my baby girl. When Mina left, she took more than a piece of my heart with her. Twelve weeks and more than a thousand hours later, here we are.

Separated, lost, heartbroken. Pregnant.

I climb the stairs to her apartment after Mina buzzes me in, her voice still thick with tears hours after she called. Her loft is a third-floor walk-up, and I feel each stair in my calves and chest as I climb them. By the time I reach her door, I'm out of breath. Panting, I knock on her door. She answers in an oversized sweatshirt, and my heart feels like it might blow up.

It's my sweatshirt.

"Uncle Grant…" she whimpers, her lips quivering as she

steps aside to let me in. I step inside the tiny apartment while she closes the door. I turn to face her and when I see the tears begin to roll down her cheeks, there's only one thing to do. I wrap my arms around her and let her cry into my shirt. Her body is wracked with sobs, and I wordlessly hold her through each one until her tears subside.

"Baby girl, maybe we should sit," I offer, guiding her into the small living room. She falls onto the couch, and I sit beside her. She tucks her legs underneath herself and puts her head in my lap. We sit quietly for a long time while I stroke her hair, whispering reassurances.

It's going to be okay. We're going to get through this. I'm not going anywhere.

When I think she's fallen asleep, Mina rolls over and looks me in the eye. There's a deep sadness in her eyes, and it pains my heart. I brush a stray curl out of her face and caress her cheek, my thumb resting across the pink bud of her lips.

"Uncle Grant, I'm scared." Her voice is hoarse from crying, her cheeks stained with mascara and tears. She's never looked more afraid. She's never looked more beautiful.

"I know, baby."

"Tell me what to do," she pleads. I take her hand in mine, bringing it to my lips. I kiss each finger and each knuckle, turning her palm over in my hand. I press another kiss into her palm and wrap her fingers around it. I've made up my mind, and there's only one answer.

"Come home with me."

"I have nowhere to go, Grant. My dad won't talk to me and—"

I cut her off, pressing a finger to her lips. "No. Come home. With me. My home is your home. It could be our home. We could raise the baby there together."

Mina looks up at me with uncertainty written all over her face, chewing her lower lip. Her eyes dart away for a moment, staring at the room around her before they land on mine once more.

"Are you sure?" Her voice is small, and she seems to recede

into herself.

"I've never been more sure of anything in my life. I've survived without you long enough. Come home. Let me take care of both of you."

"But my dad…"

"You let me worry about him. Come home, princess."

I press her fingers to my lips once more. I watch as she runs it over in her head, her eyes darting across my face. Finally, she nods, and I feel as though I can breathe again.

"Okay. I'll come home," she concedes. She looks tired and defeated, as though she's lost a great battle with herself over the decision. My heart aches for her. My heart aches for us.

We sit silently for a few moments while I stroke her cheek, brushing curls from her face. A tear rolls down her cheek, and I dry it with my shirtsleeve. She sniffles, and it tugs at the strings of my heart.

"I'm sorry," she mutters, her eyes welling up again.

"For what, baby?"

"For not telling you sooner."

"I would have come right away. I would have dropped everything. I would have—"

"I didn't want you to feel trapped, Uncle Grant. I didn't do this on purpose. I was on the pill, I swear!"

I shush her gently. "Mina, it's okay. I know you didn't. I know you'd never. I don't want you to feel, even for a moment, that this is your fault. We did this together. We made this life together. We will get through this together."

I place my hand over her belly, and she covers it with her small, delicate fingers. They intertwine with mine, and I give them a gentle squeeze.

"Come stay with me, Mina. As long as you need. As long as it takes. I'll be there every step of the way, I promise."

"Okay."

"Okay?"

"Okay. Take me home, Uncle Grant," she whispers, her eyes on our fingers. I keep my hand on her belly while she pulls away. Mina moves to sit up, and I ease her off my lap. She stands and walks around her apartment slowly, running her fingers across the back of the couch.

"I'll send someone to pack your things, baby girl. First thing in the morning." I rise from the low couch, feeling my bones creak with age. For a moment, I forgot I'm in my fifties. I forgot I'm an old man with a much younger woman. A woman now carrying my child. For a moment, I was back in college. I was young, I was full of life, I was… I was scared.

"Just take me home. Dad refuses to pay my rent or my tuition. I'm going to drop out anyway, so I may as well do it now."

My chest aches, and I reach for her, pulling her to my frame. "It's not dropping out, baby. It's withdrawing. It's taking a semester off. I won't let you throw your education away. You're going to graduate on your terms, not his."

She sniffles. I kiss her forehead, and she looks up at me, her big doe eyes welling with tears again.

"Why are you so good to me, Uncle Grant?"

The answer is simple. "Because I love you. Now, go pack a bag. We'll stay the night in a hotel, and I'll drive us home in the morning."

"We can stay here," she offers, shrugging. She rests her head against my chest, and I rub her back, gently fingering the knobby vertebrae while she relaxes into my touch.

"We can stay here, or wherever you're comfortable," I acquiesce.

"Uncle Grant?"

"Yes, princess?"

"Thank you."

"For what?"

"For coming up here. For comforting me. For not pushing me."

"I would never push you into anything you didn't want."

"I want to keep this baby," she whispers, her voice growing hoarse once more.

"There was never a question in my mind that you didn't." I pause, considering her carefully. "You look tired, princess.

Why don't you go lie down, and I'll scrounge up some dinner."

She shakes her head and looks up at me, her lip quivering. "Come with me. I don't want to be alone."

"For you, baby girl, I'll do anything. Lead the way."

Chapter Two

    I crawl into bed beside Mina, and she curls into my body, her back to my chest. We still fit together like two puzzle pieces, like the outline of states on a map. I lie on my side like California, and she presses into me like Nevada and Arizona, filling in the gaps. She pulls my arm around her while our legs intertwine, tangling like vines under the white comforter.
    I breathe in her familiar, comforting scent. Her skin still smells like gardenias with notes of peach shampoo on top. My thumb absently strokes her belly, and, within a few minutes, Mina is asleep in my arms. I listen to her breathe and feel her heartbeat echo in my chest as the rhythms sync. I haven't felt her body beside me in months, but I remember the way it feels to have her in my arms like riding a bike. I tuck my knees behind hers and kiss her shoulder while she sleeps.
    I find myself drifting off to sleep beside her, my mind stuck in the space between consciousness and sleep. I dream of our lives from this night forward. I see Mina, her belly big with our child, walking down the aisle. I see her in a white dress with flowers in her hair. The dream shifts, and I see her holding a bundle of baby wrapped in a white blanket. I see her breastfeeding, singing lullabies in a rocking chair. Every moment is a vision of Mina and the life growing inside her.
    When I wake, she's still curled in my arms, dreaming

peacefully. She looks so innocent, and I'm painfully reminded of what I've done. I stare at her as she sleeps, playing it all over in my head. I should have said no when she came on to me. I should have sent her home, I should have, I should have... It's too late to put the horse back in the barn now. I didn't do what I should have, and here we are. But also, here we are. The woman I love, curled against me, our child in her womb.

I've never been a father. Not by choice, but by circumstance. I never thought I wanted to be a father. I was selfish in my younger days, putting work ahead of my wife. I said we didn't have time to start a family. I said a lot of things I didn't mean. In the end, it left me childless and alone in an empty house. But when I look at the sleeping woman beside me and place my hand on her belly, I know I want nothing more. I want to be with Mina. I want to be a father. I want to raise this baby with her and hold them both in my arms for the rest of my life.

I don't realize I'm crying until a tear falls on Mina's cheek. I brush it away with the pad of my thumb, trying not to wake her. She stirs, and her eyes flutter open, gazing up at me through heavy lids.

"You're still here," she whispers, her voice small and unsure as she wipes the sleep from her eyes.

"I wouldn't dream of being anywhere else," I breathe, pulling her closer.

Mina looks up at me, and her brow crinkles with concern. "Have you been crying, Uncle Grant?"

"No, no, there's just some dust in my eye," I lie, hoping she buys it.

"It's okay to cry. I've been crying since I found out, too."

I caress her face with the back of my hand, searching her eyes.

"When did you find out?"

"Last month. I was late. Very late. So I bought a test at the drugstore. I wanted to call you as soon as the test came back pink, but I was scared."

"Were you alone?"

She nods, and my chest burns with each breath. I can feel my heart breaking as she tells me the story.

I should have been here with her. Guilt courses through my body, and I pull her closer.

"There was no one here to hold your hand? No one to wait with you?"

"No. I did this on my own. Every step…" Her voice trails off.

"What do you mean, 'every step'?"

"I told you to…" Her cheeks burn pink, and she casts her eyes down, staring into the small, dark space between our bodies. "I shouldn't have told you to do that."

"You wanted me to come inside you. That's not a crime, baby. It's natural, especially with someone you trust," I gently remind her.

"If I hadn't, maybe I wouldn't be…"

"Pregnant? Baby, this doesn't happen every time you have sex. I could have come inside you a hundred times and never gotten you pregnant. I could have come inside just once, and it could have happened."

"But this is all my fault," she whimpers, lip trembling. I reach up and steady her chin between my fingers, holding her gaze to mine.

"You were on the pill. You did everything right. All it takes is once. I don't regret what we did, not at all. And you shouldn't either, princess. You asked for what you wanted. You asked me to give you everything, everything you needed. I gave it to you willingly, happily, with my whole heart. Baby, I love you. I'm going to love you through this."

She blinks back a few tears and sighs. "You didn't sign up for this, Uncle Grant. You didn't sign up to be a dad. You have your own life. You don't need to be stuck with me forever."

"Listen to me, sweetheart. I'm not stuck with anything. I am here willingly. I am here freely. I'm here because I want to be. Because I want to be with you. When I spilled my seed inside you, I signed up for whatever came next." I kiss her forehead, brushing my lips over her cheek. Her hand fists in the fabric of my shirt. She runs her fingers up my chest and then tilts my chin up so my lips meet hers.

It's the first time we've kissed since that night. The first time I've tasted her. The first time I've felt her soft, baby-pink lips against mine. She presses her form against my frame with need, moaning as my tongue slips between her lips. When I pull away to catch my breath, she lets out a low whine of disappointment. I kiss her forehead and press mine against hers, drinking in the moment.

"Princess," I sigh, eyes closed. "I could do that all night. I could touch you, taste you, feel you all night. But I don't want to touch you if you don't want me. I won't ever touch you unless you want it. Your body is your own. I don't ever expect sex from you, regardless of what we shared before."

She bites her lips and nods. Her lashes flutter against my cheek as she whispers, "What if I want you to touch me?"

"Then I'll touch you. Tell me, baby. Tell me what you want, and I'll give it to you."

She's quiet for a moment, as though making up her mind. She closes her eyes and when she opens them, I see a familiar need inside them.

"I want you, Uncle Grant."

I kiss Mina as though I'm a drowning man and she's my last breath of air.

Chapter Three

I roll Mina onto her back, carefully positioning her on the pillows. I place my palm over her belly, and she reaches down, holding it there. I look down at her, and she stares back, her cheeks flushed pink.

"It's okay to touch me," she reassures. Mina squirms and lifts the hem of the sweatshirt enough to reveal her stomach. "You won't hurt us."

I kiss down her body, stopping at her bare stomach. She's tremulous at my touch, and I feel her quake as my lips press against her warm skin. My hands slide underneath her sweatshirt, and I feel her breasts for the first time in months. Reflexively, I squeeze them, kneading her soft flesh between my fingers. Mina flinches, and I immediately pull back, sitting on my heels.

"Did I hurt you?"

"No, it's okay. They're just tender." She pulls the sweatshirt over her head and drops it on the floor. Her breasts are bigger than I remember, and the nipples are a darker shade of dusty rose. I look down and see her belly, the small bump beginning to take shape. I marvel at the changes to her body, kissing my way up and down her chest. When I lave my tongue across her taut nipple, her eyes flutter, and her breath hitches in her throat. She arches her back, pressing deeper into my mouth. Her fingers rake my scalp as I flick my tongue across her plump, tender embonpoints, and she coos my name. She moans and twists her body beneath my touch as I explore her soft, warm skin.

When I nip at the stiff bud, sucking it between my teeth and clamping them around her, she yelps. I release her and look into her eyes, scanning for any signs of pain or discomfort. Mina's eyes are screwed shut, and her breath is ragged, but her fingers never leave the nape of my neck. They tighten as I shift, holding me in place.

"Do you want me to stop, baby girl? Was that too much?"

"No!" Mina's eyes shoot open in alarm, and she shakes her head. "Don't stop. Please? It feels so good, Uncle Grant."

My stomach ties in knots, hearing her call me 'uncle' in bed. It sends a chill down my spine and a rumble through my chest. Mina knows the games she's playing.

It's one thing to call me Uncle Grant when she's scared and crying in my arms. That's a matter of comforting an upset little girl.

It's another when her tits are in my mouth. This is a matter of pleasuring the woman I love. She only calls me 'Uncle Grant' like that when she wants me, and who am I to keep her from getting what she wants?

When I move my tongue across her chest from left to right in small, tight circles, she purrs like a kitten. I could suck her tits all day. I'll never be tired of listening to her love sounds and feeling the way her body reacts. I take great satisfaction in the way she blossoms under my ministrations and the way she unfurls beneath my kiss. She opens her body to me, and I want to bury myself inside her.

"I want more," she pleads. I pull away from her taut, darkened tits and look her in the eyes, seeing the need burning inside them.

"Lift your hips, princess. Let me see that pretty pussy."

I tie my fingers into the waistband of her black leggings and gently tug them down. I remove her panties and drop them on the floor with the rest of her clothes. Once Mina is bare in front of me, my heart begins to race. I've never seen her look more beautiful. The gentle slope of her growing belly draws me in like a magnet, and I kiss my way across the soft skin. Her body is a marvel I could admire all day. The changes that have taken place over the last twelve weeks are mystifying, captivating, and phenomenal, and I can't get enough.

I kiss my way down her belly to the downy hair of her mound, burying my face in her. She smells like sweat and desire. Looking up the length of her body, I cup her mound and slide a finger inside her cleft while I study her face. Mina shuts her eyes and takes a deep breath, anticipating my next move. I circle my tongue around her clit, and she arches, parting her legs more. I run my tongue over the taut nub, flicking and sucking as she squirms and bucks her hips. I slowly slip one digit inside her, curling and uncurling my finger as I play with her.

Her legs tighten around my head, and she lets out a soft yelp. I look up at her, studying her for signs of pain or discomfort. Slowly, her eyes flutter open, and she looks down at me, her hazy eyes focusing on my face.

"Why did you stop?" Her voice is thick with need, and, for a moment, I feel guilty for depriving her of pleasure.

"I need you to tell me if it's too much."

"It'll never be too much. More. Oh God, give me more."

"As you wish."

Her body warms up to my touch, and she shudders as I toy with her. Mina grinds her hips against my hand, trying to take my fingers deeper. Her core contracts around my digits as they slide through her tight wetness. She moans and whimpers my name as her pleasure begins to build. I can feel the orgasm beginning to bubble up inside, waiting to burst like a cork. Mina shifts her hips to accommodate my fingers and when I slide them in and out, her body convulses with pleasure.

"More. Please, more." Any shred of uncertainty flees my brain as I push into her with my thick fingers. I've never felt her this wet, this ready, this needy. Her cunt is hot and sticky around my digits, and I know I'll be smelling her scent on them for days. She purrs like a kitten when I stroke her walls and thumb her clit in tandem. I watch with satisfaction as she undulates and twitches beneath my touch. She's so fucking beautiful when she rides my hand like this. I want more, more, more. I want all she has to give me. I want to give her all I have in return. All I want is my Mina.

When I slide my tongue over the swollen tip of her pretty, pink nub, she shatters beneath me. One stroke and all her walls come crashing down. She cries out my name, locks her legs around my shoulders, and holds me to her pussy. I give my princess everything she wants and more as my tongue glides along her sopping slit and my fingers curl along her walls. She arches her back and digs her heels into my shoulder blades, pinning me in place.

I slide my free hand up her belly and rest it over the growing bump, feeling the power surge through her body. Her juices coat my face as she comes, dribbling down my chin onto my shirt. I feel her stomach tighten as the pleasure rolls through her. She tenses, and her sharp heels scrape my skin. Her fingers knot in the sheets, and her knuckles turn white as she rides the wave of her orgasm. Mina's body releases its tension as I slide my fingers out and trace the sweet, sticky love dripping down my lips. She tastes like honey. She tastes like sunshine. She tastes like home.

I crawl up her body to rest beside her, stroking her cheek and whispering love words in her ear as she recovers. I pull the sheet over her naked body, trying to keep her warm. After a few quiet moments when I'm sure she's asleep, Mina rolls over to face me, her growing belly between us. I place my hand over it, massaging the taut skin. I trace the lines of her fledgling stretchmarks, marveling at the changes taking place.

Mina looks up at me with her big, emerald doe eyes full of questions. She stares into my eyes, licking her lip nervously. I take her small hand in mine and intertwine our fingers. I bring our hands to my lips and kiss her knuckles.

"Uncle Grant?"

"Yes, baby?"

Her voice is small and scared. "Do you still love me?"

"I've never loved you more."

There's a long pause between us, and then, "Will you stay with me?"

"Wild horses couldn't pull me away," I reassure her as I kiss her forehead.

She nuzzles into my shoulder as I run my hand over her belly and back. Within a few moments, she's asleep. I draw the blanket over her shoulders and drift off, my mind playing the same words over and over again.

Nothing will ever keep me away from you again, princess.

Chapter Four

In the morning, Mina and I wake slowly. Wrapped in my arms, her body warm with comfort and sleep in her eyes, I take my time getting out of bed. I kiss her forehead, her cheeks, and her neck while her fingers tangle in the dark hair on my chest. They weave in and out as she rakes her nails over my skin. We lie in bed for what feels like hours without saying a word. It's unadulterated bliss, and I never want this morning to end.

Midday comes far too soon, and we have to make the long drive back to the city and back home. I make arrangements to have her apartment packed and stored while Mina loads her luggage with clothes and necessities. Within a few hours, her bag is packed, her apartment is closed up until Monday, and we're on the road.

By the time we reach the city, Mina is asleep in the passenger seat. She looks so innocent in her slumber that I can't bear to wake her when we arrive. I park and quietly open the door, dashing up the drive to unlock the house. I sneak back to the car, open the passenger door, and silently unclip her from her seatbelt. Sliding my arms under her, I carry Mina into the house, careful not to jostle her too much.

Halfway into the living room, I hear her tiny, sleepy words mumbling against my chest.

"Are we home?"

"Yes, princess. Do you want to go back to sleep?"

"No. I can walk." I gently ease her to her feet. Mina stumbles forward on shaky legs, and I reach out to steady her. I wrap my arm around her waist and pull our bodies close. She relaxes into my touch and leans against me, her chest to my back. Her head lolls against my shoulder as she takes my hand and puts it on her belly.

"I thought I dreamed it all." Her voice is low, slow, and tinged with sleepiness. I kiss the top of her head and nuzzle her hair. I can feel the sleep radiating off of her in waves through the warmth of her skin.

"What all?" I whisper, watching our reflection in the great mirror in front of us. My hand on her belly, her body pressed to mine—it's like a dream. Late afternoon light filters in, painting the room in an orange, creamy haze.

"This. You."

"It's not a dream, baby. I'm here," I reassure her. She clasps my hand that's laying over her belly, intertwining our fingers. We rock side to side, silently, for a long time. I bury my face in her shoulder, relishing the quiet and trying not to break the spell.

"Grant, where am I going to stay? Here, I mean?"

I hadn't considered her staying anywhere other than with me, in my room. In my bed. I want to keep Mina by my side always, but I know that's not possible. She needs room to breathe, and I won't keep her cooped up. I won't lock her away like a princess in a storybook. Mina is a grown woman, and she can make her own choices.

I gesture to the house. "Anywhere you want. I'll give you your own room if you'd like. Or…" I pause, swallowing the lump in my throat. "Or you can stay with me. The choice is yours. I don't want you to feel like you have to…"

"Can I sleep alone tonight?" Her voice is soft, uncertain, and vulnerable.

My heart seems to crack, but I nod and plaster a brave look on my face. I've already resolved to give Mina everything she wants. Even if it's her own space.

"Anything you want, sweetheart. I'll have the guest room made up for you. I'll put towels in the bathroom and—"

She interrupts me, her words tumbling out like a fountain. "Thank you. I don't want to seem ungrateful, it's just that I…" She trails off and stares at the ground. "It's not that I want to be alone tonight. I don't want to feel like I'm intruding on your space."

"You're not intruding on anything, baby girl. It's your home now, too. It's our home."

Mina turns in my arms and wraps her hands around the back of my neck. She rises on tiptoe and kisses my cheek, her lashes fluttering against my skin.

"Thank you for understanding," she whispers, her voice soft in the shell of my ear.

"Always, sweetheart. Now, make yourself at home. I'll bring in your bag while you make yourself comfortable."

Mina sinks onto her heels and releases her hold on me, a soft, shy smile playing over her features.

"I don't know my way around yet. I've only been upstairs, remember?"

Oh, do I remember…

"I'll give you a tour once I've brought your stuff in. There's more than just a foyer and my bedroom, I promise."

Mina's cheeks flush strawberry pink, and I kiss her forehead. "I'll be right back," I assure her, squeezing her fingers before I turn for the door.

When I return from bringing in her bags, Mina is already asleep on the couch. With her legs tucked under her and her hand over her belly, she looks like an angel on Earth. I smile softly as I take her in from the doorway. This is my life now, I muse to myself. I cross the doorway into the room and pull a blanket from behind the couch, draping it over her. I settle into the leather chair opposite her and drift off as I listen to her steady breathing.

This is my life now.

Chapter Five

After giving her the space she requested, a room of her own at the end of the hall, Mina settles into life in my—our—home easily. I give her carte blanche over decorating and furnishing the room as she sees fit and within a week, she feels more at home. Her furniture is brought from her apartment in Connecticut, and she has the room painted a sweet, butter yellow. It brightens up the space and brings color into my usually drab, grey, monotonous life. Mina breathes new life into my old bones, even though she refuses to stay in my bed at night. I promised to give her space, even if it means not having her in my arms.

I decide to officially resign from my position as CEO of Wolf Industries, handing the reins over to the board to find my successor. I don't care who runs Wolf, so long as they don't run it into the ground. Any one of the board of directors would be more than qualified to take over, and I tell them as much. When I'm not hammering out the details of my resignation, I find myself spending more and more time at home. I find little reasons to stick around the house, pretending to be working when, in reality, I'm watching her.

I steal glimpses of Mina in the kitchen, fixing her daily lemon tea and toast. I hear her in the shower, singing to herself. I catch her napping on the chaise in my office some afternoons, and she looks too peaceful to wake. I forgot what it was like to have another heartbeat in the house after all those years alone. In fact, I have two new heartbeats in our home. I watch as her belly grows incrementally, noting the changes in her body with awe. It amazes me to know the life she's carrying inside of her is a life we made together.

At sixteen weeks, she invites me to a prenatal checkup. I've never been to one, and I don't know what to expect. We sit in uncomfortable plastic chairs in a tiny waiting room, and my knee bounces with nervous energy. Gently, Mina reaches out and places her hand on my thigh.

"It's going to be all right, Grant," she says, her voice sweet like honey. She soothes my nerves as she tucks her small hand in mine, squeezing my fingers. She provides peace I didn't know was possible, and, in the moment, I know she's right. I kiss her cheek, and she squeezes again, reassuring me.

The medical assistant calls us back, and I follow Mina into the office, taking a seat beside her as the MA runs her blood pressure and asks questions about the pregnancy. Mina smiles at me as she answers them, her hand never leaving mine. They draw blood. I've never been squeamish, but my stomach flips watching them stick a needle in her arm. To her credit, Mina takes it like a champ, and I've never been prouder of her in my life.

When it's time for the ultrasound, my heart jumps into my throat, and I stand, ready to leave the room and give Mina and the technician their privacy. It's my turn to not want to intrude. I rise from the stool, straighten my shirt, and move for the door. I'm two feet from the bed when Mina tugs on my shirt, turning me around to face her.

"Stay. Please?" Mina's voice is soft. Her eyes find mine, scanning my face for any sign of uncertainty, and I push every thought of bolting out of my head. I sit beside her again as she lifts her shirt, and the ultrasound technician slathers her in jelly. Mina winces and giggles uncomfortably, and I look at her with worry.

"It's just cold."

OLIVE SPENCER

A few moments later, I hear our child's heartbeat for the first time. I stare at the screen in awe while Mina holds my hand. Tears well up in my eyes, and I realize I haven't cried in years. Mina looks over at me softly and lovingly brushes them from my cheek with the tips of her fingers. I watch as a blob the size of an eclair comes into focus, moving and shifting on the screen.

"Congratulations, Dad. It's a baby."

I break down into sobs at that point, and the technician is kind enough to pass me a box of tissues while I recompose myself. Mina squeezes my hand while she and the tech talk, laughing softly at a joke I don't hear. The sound of our child's heartbeat echoes in my head, and I've never heard anything more wonderful.

The tech prints out a set of sonogram photos and sends us on our way, telling Mina to stop and schedule her next appointment on the way out. I tell her I'll pull the car around, and she tucks one of the sonograms into my pocket. I try to hold back more tears as I make my way through the sliding doors and into the parking lot. I finger the image in my pocket and pull it out as I slide into the driver's seat.

I've never seen anything more beautiful. It's only a black-and-white blob, but it contains my entire world. Everything I have, everything I'll ever be, is right in front of me on a shiny sheet of paper. I tuck the photo into the corner of my dash and pull the car around as Mina walks outside. She slides into the passenger seat and closes the door.

"How do you feel?" she asks softly as she pulls the seatbelt over her chest and clicks it in place.

My voice wavers as I find the words. "I never thought I could feel this way. I'm so in love." I sigh. Her small hand finds mine on the shifter, her thumb circling my knuckles.

"That's how I felt the first time I heard it, too. I didn't know my heart was big enough to love like this."

"I didn't think mine was either until you came into my life, Mina," I confess. I feel her eyes on my face as I pull out onto the street. She's quiet for a long time, and I catch her staring out the window, looking pensive. She pulls her hand back into her own lap and I miss the feel of her skin on mine instantaneously. It's the longest contact we've had in weeks; if I'd known it would be over so soon, I would've paid more attention.

I focus on the drive home, my eyes on the road. I know if I bring myself to look at Mina, I'll never look away. I want her. I need her. I crave her. It's been weeks since she crawled into my bed late at night, wrapping her arms around me and pulling me close. I haven't felt her warm body beside me in so long, I forgot what it's like to wake up in a bed that isn't ice cold. We live like roommates, not like lovers. I promised to give her space but if I'd known it would be like this, I would have fought harder. I would have held her longer. I would have kissed her deeper. I would have loved her sweeter. I would have... I would have.

We arrive at our house, and I pull into the garage, parking the car in the usual spot. I shut off the engine and lean back in the seat, closing my eyes for a moment as I replay the events of the afternoon. Mina opens the door and rushes out, and I'm afraid I've done something to upset her. I grip the steering wheel and rest my head against it, cursing under my breath. A moment later, my door opens, and Mina pushes me back in my chair.

She moves the seat, and I slide backward, watching her curiously. She puts a finger to my lips when I begin to question her, silencing me with a look. Mina doesn't say a word as she slides onto my lap and puts my hand on her belly. She wraps her arms around my neck and brings my face to hers, our lips meeting in the middle. I close my eyes and let her take control, giving in to the moment.

When she breaks away, her eyes are dark with lust. She runs the tip of her tongue along the curve of her lower lip, staring wordlessly into my eyes. She grabs my hand, still resting on her belly, and brings it to her breast, forcing me to palm it through the thin fabric of her shirt.

"I need you. Now. I need to feel you moving inside me. I

need to feel you filling me full of cum. I need to hear you call me a good girl while I suck your cock. It's been so long, Uncle Grant. Fuck me. Don't make love to me. Fuck. Me."

I look her in the eyes, searching for signs of hesitation or uncertainty. She stares back at me, eyes lit from within with desire. She runs her fingers up the nape of my neck and presses her lips to my ear, her voice low as it rumbles inside my head.

"Didn't you hear me? I said, 'Fuck me, Uncle Grant.'"

I swallow the lump in my throat as my arms tighten around her waist, pressing her body to mine. I finger her nipple, feeling it pebble beneath my touch as I whisper in her ear.

"Yes, princess."

Chapter Six

 By the time we reach her room, I've tasted Mina on every flat surface between it and the front door. I've kissed her in every doorway, pressed her against every wall, and pinned her arms overhead enough times to leave red marks on my knuckles. I've stripped her of all but her panties as she collapses onto the bed in a breathless, panting heap.
 I stand over her, loosening my belt and slipping it through the loops of my trousers in one smooth motion. She rests on her elbows and stares up at me with hunger and desire in her eyes as I unzip and let the fabric fall to my feet. She reaches forward and pushes open the flap in my boxers, freeing my ramrod-hard cock. I shudder as I look down and see the wanton lust in her eyes. Mina sits up and runs her fingertip down the length of my shaft and back again, teasing me with each pass. She rubs the pad of her thumb around my swollen, pink tip, already damp with precum, and sucks it into her mouth.
 I watch as her eyes close in bliss while she sucks my dripping love from her digit. She moans, and the sound drives a bolt of lightning straight through my cock. I rake my fingers through her red, messy curls and tilt her head up until our eyes meet. She slowly slides her thumb out of her mouth with a slick, wet pop and blinks up at me sweetly. Her hand wraps around my

length and begins to slide along it, picking up the pace with each movement. Her gaze never leaves mine until I shut my eyes in ecstasy. It's been so long since she touched me this way, and I know I won't last. I try to slide out of her grip, and she tightens her fist at the base.

"No." Her voice is firm, and I don't dare move. She holds my whole world in the palm of her hand. I willingly give myself over to Mina, letting her take control of my immediate future. Tilting my head forward, my eyes open slowly, and I stare down at my precious girl as she opens wide. Her bubblegum-pink tongue coats my shaft in hot, sticky saliva while she takes me into her mouth. I feel my eyes roll into the back of my head as she begins to bob her head, softly moaning with each pass over the tip.

I've never felt such divine ecstasy. Mina sucks my cock like it's the last one she'll ever see, putting her whole head into it. I push her curls out of her face and tighten my grip at the nape of her neck while she works her magic.

"Good girl. Good girl."

I shudder and curse as my pleasure builds, whimpering her name and begging her not to stop. Pinpricks of satisfaction being to tingle my spine, and I slide out of Mina's hot, wet mouth with a deep groan.

Mina looks up at me with her big doe eyes and whimpers, pleading without saying a word. I know she wants this as badly as I do. I can read her body like a book, even now. Her cheeks are the color of carnations, and her belly trembles with each labored breath. Her eyes burn with desire, and she squirms, trying to ease the ache between her thighs. Even now, with new life growing inside her, I know the sure-fire signs of lust radiating from Mina's body. Nothing has changed in the months since I've felt myself inside of her.

I recover my breath, and she reaches greedily for my cock. I step far enough away that she can't reach, and Mina pouts, sticking her lower lip out like a toddler. She crosses her arms over her chest, and I step toward her. I stroke her cheek with my finger, chuckling at her.

"Is that any way to get what we want, princess?" I tease. My hard cock dances in front of her face, twitching with need. She licks her lips and uncrosses her arms, staring up at me expectantly.

"Please?"

"Please, what? What do you want from me, baby?"

Mina runs her palm up my hip to my belly, then along the planes of my chest. Her fingers tangle in the downy hair as she rakes her nails over my skin. Powerful shivers course through me, and Mina smirks up at me. She's got me in the palm of her hand now, and I know it. There's not a thing on earth I wouldn't give her.

She looks up at me with her big doe eyes. "I want to use me, Uncle Grant. I want you to break me. I want you to fuck me."

"Oh, God," I moan as her words wash over me. Use her. Break her. Fuck her.

Mina scoots back onto the bed, hooks her fingers in the waistband of her panties, and slides them down her legs. She kicks them across the room as she slides her hand between her legs and pushes her knees apart. Mina bares her slick, juicy, baby-pink pussy to the world, and the scent of her arousal sparks a fire inside me. I push my boxers down my thighs and tear off my shirt, throwing them on the floor. I close in on Mina, and she sinks deeper into her bedding.

My cock waits at the entrance to her sex, tapping the soft flesh and dribbling down her pink slit. I pin her arms above her head and stare down into her eyes. Passion burns in them, and I know this is exactly what my baby girl wants. This is exactly what she needs. I sink my length inside the velvet sheath of her hot pussy, and the world explodes around me.

It's been so long since I've been buried to the hilt inside her. Her warmth wraps around me like a glove as I thrust. Mina rocks her hips into mine, moaning with every move. The sound of her pleasure is music to my ears. Her need drives my thrusts deeper and faster as the unmistakable high of my climax creeps up on me. When I unsheathe myself from within her, Mina cries out in anguish.

I shush her softly, cooing in her ear. "Easy, precious. We're just getting started. Let me catch my breath."

Mina turns her head, and our lips meet in a searing kiss. Her mouth is hungry and greedy, and she claims me as her own with each pass of her tongue over mine. She pulls me on top of her and as we recline into the bed, she shifts uncomfortably. She grimaces and arches her back, trying to wiggle loose.

"What's wrong, baby?"

She shifts again and pulls something from behind her back. Mina tries to tuck it under the sheets, but my hand darts out and reaches for it, pinning her in place. Her fingers clench into a fist, obscuring the object as she tries to wrestle her arm free from my grasp. I pin her tighter until she releases her grip, and I pluck the object from her palm.

It's a small, pink vibrator. I smirk at Mina, and she eyes me sheepishly. She casts her eyes down, and heat blossoms across the apples of her cheeks.

"Is this how you've been keeping busy, baby girl?" I hold the vibrator between us, pressing the button and turning it on. A steady thrum fills the air between us, and she blinks up at me, almost innocently.

"Have you been keeping yourself locked away from me, playing with your toys every night? Tell me, princess. When you use this magic wand, does it feel as good as my tongue between your thighs? Do you cry out for it when you come in the middle of the night, or is it my name on your lips?"

Mina looks up at me and licks her lips. "I use it every night. It's the only thing that keeps me from crawling into your bed."

I press the vibrator to the apex between her thighs, and she shudders, her body coiling at the intense vibrations. I cup my palm around her mound and hold the toy in place as I lean over, drawing my tongue over the shell of her ear.

"You should be crawling into my bed. You should be bringing your toys and showing your dear Uncle Grant how you like to play with yourself. Why don't you show me now." My voice is low in her ear, commanding. I pull the toy back and run it along her dripping slit, circling her entrance slowly before tucking it into my palm.

"Please, Uncle Grant..." Mina whimpers as I press my palm against her body. The vibrator pulses, and she squirms to get out of my touch. My free hand clenches around her thigh, holding her in place.

"What's that, baby girl? Speak up. I can't hear you over the sound of your toy."

"Please!" she cries out as I drag it over her clit, her body convulsing with need.

"Yes, baby girl. Show your uncle how you touch yourself."

Chapter Seven

I slide down Mina's body, kissing my way over her silky skin as she moves into a comfortable position. I sit on my heels at the foot of the bed, watching her twist and move. Her growing belly rises and falls with each breath, and her breasts sway gently as she reclines into a nest of pillows. She parts her legs, baring herself to me once more. Turning on the vibrator, she slowly rubs it along her slit, parting her folds. She shudders as it makes contact with her clit, and her breath hitches in her throat. A soft moan escapes her lips as she begins to play.

Sitting on my knees, I watch, rapt. Mina spreads her folds and drags the vibrator around the taut nub and slips it into her slit. She pumps her fingers, pushing and pulling and whimpering as she pleasures herself. One hand on her pussy, one hand tweaking her nipple, I've never seen her look sexier. I want to ravish her. I want to make soft love to her. I want to bury my dick in her and never pull out. She's everything I could ever want, everything I could ever need.

Her legs twitch and shake as she picks up the pace, and her head lolls back against the pillows. I catch her breath speeding up, and I know her orgasm is near.

"That's it, princess. That's my girl. Show me how you come. Don't hold back," I coo, stroking my cock as I watch her hips undulate. Mina rocks her hips and flicks her finger rapidly across her taut, dark nipple. Pleasure begins to build at the base of my spine, bubbling and boiling within. I know I won't last long, listening to her moans and watching her toy slip and slide in and out of her dripping cunt. I can smell her musk, and it makes my mouth water.

Mina pulls the toy out of her pussy and presses it directly on her swollen clit. She gasps and writhes under its vibrations, and I know she's close. I crawl on my knees toward her, and she parts her legs to let me in. I rush to come with her, furiously pumping my hand over my dick. We're going to come together. I'm going to shoot my load over her swollen belly, I'm so close to her now.

"Come for me, baby. I need you to come." My voice is hoarse with want, and Mina nods, her eyes still screwed shut with pleasure. I kneel in front of her, stroking and squeezing my cock with all my strength, waiting for her to come undone before me. Her hand bounces off the tip of my cock as she works the toy over. When her knees rise and lock me in their grasp, I know she's going to climax.

"Grant!" She cries out my name, and my cum explodes from within, shooting thick, hot ropes over her belly. She jolts, and her hips buck as she holds the toy in place, letting the burst of pleasure overtake her. Our shared release is powerful and as it courses through my body, I lose control of my brain. The words slip out of my mouth before I realize what I'm saying.

"Marry me, princess."

"Yes!"

I collapse beside her, spent. Her body still shivers with release beside me, but it soon wanes, and she stills. I lay next to her, listening to her breathe, watching her chest as her pounding heartbeat slows and returns to normal. My cum drips down the curve of her belly, coating her in creamy, white strings. I feel a pang of guilt for covering her in my love like this, but the thought is replaced by the realization of what I've just asked her.

I jolt upright and stare at her in disbelief. "Baby... Did you just agree to marry me?"

OLIVE SPENCER

Mina is quiet, but her eyes find mine as she comes back to earth. They're hazy and lovestruck as they pass over my face. She props herself up on her elbows and slides backward until she rests against the headboard. I turn over and cage her between my arms, holding her in place.

Her voice is soft, barely above a whisper. "Yes."

"Yes?" My heart begins to beat out of my chest, and my mouth goes dry.

She nods, drawing her eyes up my body as a small smile turns up the corner of her rosebud lips.

"Yes. I'll marry you, Grant."

I take her into my arms, rolling her on top of me as I kiss her face, neck, and forehead. I've never felt so full of life. I've never felt so full of love. She giggles as we roll around on the bed. She's on top of me, staring down at me with stars in her eyes. Her cheeks are flushed, and her messy, red curls fall around her face. She's never been more beautiful to me.

Reverentially, I run my fingers up her sticky belly, feeling the life growing inside her. The life we made. The life we created from nothing but our love. I kiss the space between her breasts as I palm her taut skin.

"Let's do it, baby. Let's do it today. I don't want to wait a minute longer." My voice is soft and low, in that bedroom tone I know she can't resist. She stares into my eyes, scanning my face.

"Are you sure?"

"I've never been more sure of anything in my life. Marry me, princess. Marry me today."

She leans over me and drops her mouth to the shell of my ear. I shiver as her hot breath spreads over my skin, leaving a trail of goosebumps up my arm.

"Let's get married, Uncle Grant. I don't want to wait. I want to be yours forever."

"You're already mine forever, baby."

"Then let's make it official."

She kisses my cheek and rolls over onto the bed. She looks at me with love in her eyes as she whispers, "We'll have to get cleaned up first."

"No. Get dressed. I want to marry you with my cum dried on your belly. You're mine, baby girl. Mine forever."

I turn on my side and kiss her, cupping her chin with my palm. She breaks away breathlessly and caresses my cheek as her eyes focus on mine.

"Yes, Uncle Grant," she acquiesces.

"Good girl. Now get dressed before I fuck you senseless. The longer we sit here, the more I want you again. And you know I always get what I want." I kiss her forehead before she slides out of bed. I watch her retreating form as she pads across the carpet to her closet.

Mina is my past, present, and future, and I can't wait for that future to begin.

Chapter Eight

I dress in a hurry, finding a clean, pressed button-down and slacks. Part of me says to wear a suit and make a spectacle of the occasion, but the larger voice in my head says to be casual, to play it cool. My heart thumps in my chest, and my hands shake as I wait at the foot of the stairs for Mina to emerge. The minutes tick by. I imagine she's trying to find the perfect dress. I don't know what she has in her closet. I don't know if she even likes to wear dresses. I've only seen her in a dress once, on a night that changed the course of our lives.

I wait a few moments longer before tiptoeing up the staircase and creeping into her bedroom. I spy her standing naked in front of the mirror, holding a flowing, white dress over her growing belly. Her shoulders shake, and her head is downturned. With one look, I know something is wrong.

"Baby?"

She startles and turns, dropping the dress. Her cheeks are pink, and her eyes are puffy from crying. I rush to her, wrapping my arms around her as I pull her into my chest.

"What's wrong, princess? Tell me. Tell me how I can fix it."

"I'm too fat."

"What?"

"I'm too fat to wear my dress," she moans. She sounds so despondent; it nearly breaks my heart. My everything, my only thing, my Mina. She's never been fat a day in her life, and now she has life growing inside her. I can only imagine the mental challenges of adjusting to that growth, in addition to the physical change.

I stroke her back, cooing reassurances in her ear while her tears stain my shirt. Her body continues to shake as she sobs, and my heart feels as though it might break in two. I never want to see her cry. I never want to see her hurt. There's nothing I wouldn't do, nothing I wouldn't say, to cheer her up and dry those tears.

I bring my lips to her ear, murmuring soft words of comfort. "You're growing our child inside you, baby girl. You're creating an entirely new human inside your womb. You're not fat. You're the most beautiful woman I've ever seen." I kiss the top of her head while she hiccups. "You don't need to wear white today, princess. You can wear whatever color you'd like."

"But I want to wear this dress! I bought it—" She hiccups, jolting in my arms. "I bought it a long time ago. I always wanted to be—" Another hiccup rocks her frame, and I hold her tighter. "I always wanted to be married in this dress."

I stroke her hair and tilt her chin up until her gaze meets mine. I brush away a stray tear from her round, pink cheeks. She looks away and I tilt her face back to mine.

"Look at me, Mina."

"I can't." Her eyes are dark with tears, and her usual bright-eyed sparkle has been dulled. It pains me to see her so miserable, so downtrodden.

I wait for her eyes to find mine before speaking. "Princess, I will give you everything. Everything you've ever wanted. If that means waiting until you fit into your dream dress to marry you, then I will wait. I'll wait as long as that takes."

She blinks at me, her eyes still watery. "But you said you can't wait to spend forever with me."

"Baby girl, I'm already going to spend forever with you. I'm going to spend every day of the rest of our lives with you. Loving you. Growing with you. Growing old with you."

A weak chuckle escapes her lips, and a small smile turns up

the corner of her mouth. "Uncle Grant, you're already old."

I chuckle. "Fine. Growing older with you. We have all the time in the world, baby girl. If today's not the day, there will be plenty of other days in the future."

Mina sniffles and wipes her eyes with the palms of her hands. She leans her head on my chest and breathes deeply as another hiccup wracks her frame. Mina takes my hand and places it over her belly. We hold hands over the life she's growing, and everything feels right in the world.

She looks up at me, sniffling once more. "Thank you."

"For what, baby girl?"

"For everything."

I rub her belly and kiss her forehead, my lips lingering against her skin. I close my eyes and absorb the moment until I feel her shift in my arms. My eyes open, and I watch as she turns, her belly pressing into my hips. Mina wraps her arms around my neck and rises on tiptoe, kissing my cheek.

"Let's get married, Uncle Grant. Let's do it right now."

I smile, and a chuckle passes my lips. "We can't get married until you get dressed."

"I don't need to get dressed. I don't need a slip of paper to prove my love for you, Uncle Grant. I don't need anything else. I don't need anyone else. All I need is you." She strokes my cheek, her fingers skittering across my stubble as I search her face.

She's not wrong. We don't need a slip of paper. We don't need anything.

"It's unorthodox," I start, but she cuts me off with her finger to my lips.

"Nothing about us is orthodox. Just say yes." Mina's big, green eyes search my face, pleading with me without saying a thing.

I smile and wrap my arms around her waist, lifting her off her tiptoes.

"Yes, baby girl. Yes."

She grins and covers my face in kisses. Happy tears spring to my eyes, and she wipes them away.

"I've never been married before, Uncle Grant. I don't know what to do next."

"Don't worry. I have. I know what to do."

Slowly, I lower her to her feet, feeling her body slide down mine. I cup her round tummy and drop to my knees, kissing my way across the taut, pink skin.

I take Mina's hand in mine as I kneel, gazing at her. "I, Grant Clarke Wolf, take you, Wilhelmina Evelyn Maguire, to be my wife. I take you in sickness and in health, for richer or for poorer, until death do we part. I give you everything I am, and everything I will ever be."

A tear rolls down her cheek. She sniffles and wipes her face with her free hand.

I continue. "I give you my love, my life, my heart, and my home. Wherever you go, I go. Whatever you do, I do with you. From this moment on, you are never alone." I rise to my full height, stand before her, and cup her chin in my palm. "It's your turn, baby girl."

She whispers, her eyes wide. "What do I say?"

"Whatever comes from the heart."

Mina takes a deep breath. "I, Wilhelmina Maguire, take you, Grant Wolf, to be my husband, now, and always. I choose you over everyone and everything else in my life. Father of my child, I give you my heart, my body, my soul. I love you today, tomorrow, and every day that follows."

I lower my lips to her ear. "I love you, Mina. With this, I take you as my wife."

I kiss her, and Mina melts into my arms, sighing contentedly. She kisses me back, pressing her naked body into mine, and I feel her nipples harden through the fabric of my shirt.

I pull back, grinning as I take in the sight of her. Mina, my everything, my only thing, my wife. I'm positively giddy, both at the word and at the realization that she's mine forever.

"Come to bed with me, baby."

"Ready again so soon?"

"Oh, no. This isn't about me. This is about you. My new bride. My wife. Let me take you to bed and worship you from head to toe."

"And how do you plan to do that?" She giggles, and the sound shatters me. She's so happy, she's so beautiful, and the best part of all? She's mine.

"I have a few ideas, princess. Get your ass in my bed. Now."

She waddles off toward my room, her hips swaying. She stops in the doorway and looks back over her shoulder.

"Aren't you coming, Uncle Grant?"

"I'm not, baby, but you will be," I growl, closing the gap between us in three swift strides. I lean down and snatch Mina into my arms. She tightens her grip around my shoulder, giggling as I carry her down the hall. What kind of husband would I be if I didn't carry my bride across the threshold?

Chapter Nine

Mina giggles as I drop her onto my bed, depositing her in the middle of the cloud of comforters and pillows. She looks angelic surrounded by the puffy white fabric, and her body calls to me like a siren song. I kick off my shoes as I crawl up the bed, positioning myself between her legs. I've never been able to get enough of Mina, not since the first time I tasted her kiss and felt her tight cunt gripping my cock like a glove. She's my one weakness, and she knows it.

She parts her thighs and props up on her elbows as I close in on her. I kneel between her legs and grab her wrists, pulling them overhead and caging her between my hands. My fingers knot in the pillows beneath her head as I gaze hungrily at her body. My eyes trail over her curves and planes, and I lick my lips. She pretends to struggle, but we both know this is an act. Mina loves it when I take control. She loves it when I show her who's boss.

I tighten my grip on her wrists as she flexes her fingers. I lower my lips to the shell of her ear. I breathe in, inhaling her familiar scent, and growl as it washes over me. Sex, sweat, gardenias. The perfect perfume for my perfect princess. My beautiful bride.

I release one wrist, then clasp my gigantic mitt over both of them, holding her in place as my free hand begins to explore. I stroke her cheek, cup her chin, and trail my index finger down her sternum. Mina shivers and sighs beneath me, her hips rocking against mine. She's so needy. I'll never get tired of the way her body reacts to the sound of my voice, to the simplest of my touches.

"Have I told you how beautiful you are, baby? How much I love the delicate slope of your belly and the gentle sway of your breasts?"

Mina shakes her head, her dark green eyes lit with desire. I watch as she bites her lower lip while her eyes scan my face. "No, I don't think you have. Not lately."

"Then let me remind you."

I cup her breast in my large palm, kneading her soft, warm flesh. They're so large, so full now. One breast barely fits in my palm without spilling out, and it drives me crazy. I love watching her chest heave with every breath. I kiss along the side, dragging my tongue along the sloping curve of her fullness.

She whimpers as my fingers brush over her tight, darkened nipple. I flick my index finger over the taut bud and spit on it, rubbing it in. Her eyes go wide, and a gasp falls from her lips, but Mina doesn't try to escape. She tips her head back and closes her eyes as I wrap my lips around her engorged tit, circling my tongue. When I suction the sweet little nub, she dribbles into my mouth, and I pull back in surprise. Mina's eyes fly open, and her cheeks burn red.

"Fuck! Let me go! Get off me!"

She pulls her hands out of my grasp and sits up suddenly, covering herself with her hands. I sit up and laugh, licking my lips. She tastes salty, but I like it. I didn't know she could do that. I didn't even know that was possible. But now that I know? I'm hungry for more.

"That's a neat trick, baby girl. Can you do it again?"

She looks at me with surprise. "'You... liked that?"

"I did. I didn't know you could do that, princess. Have you done that before?" She looks down, shutting her eyes. I stroke her cheek. "There's nothing to be ashamed of, Mina. Not between us. Not anymore."

Her voice is gentle and uncertain when she finds it.

"Do you..." She pauses, swallows, and then focuses her eyes on me. "Do you want to keep going?" Her eyes scan my face, and I scoot closer, parting her thighs slowly. I trail a line of kisses along her collarbone as one hand cups her mound. Mina moans as I press a finger inside her folds and circle her clit.

"Does this feel good to you, baby?"

She's quiet, her breath coming out ragged as I continue toying with her. Her tits heave as she rocks her hips into my hand. Sliding into her, I pump my fingers hard and fast until Mina is panting.

"I said, does it feel good, baby?

"It feels really good."

"Do you want me to suck on your tits, baby girl? Do you want me to finger your sweet pussy and suck your tits at the same time?" Mina blinks a few times, her mouth hanging open in a soft 'o.' Slowly, she nods and slides back, reclining. With her legs spread wide, her cheeks burn even redder as she moves her hand, revealing her swollen breasts. Creamy, white droplets cling to her dark nipples in stunning contrast. Slowly, she brings her fingers up her pendulous breast and manipulates the swollen bud.

Mina jiggles her breasts, manipulating them with her palms and fingers. She pushes them together, spreads them apart, and makes them sway when she releases them. I stare, rapt, at the way they move. Her tits have always been fantastic, but now? They're even more phenomenal.

I continue to massage her dripping pussy. Her core clenches, gripping me tight. Mina whimpers when I withdraw and drag them through her slick. Her head tilts forward to watch me through bedroom eyes while I reposition myself. The mattress shifts and creaks as I push closer, spreading her thighs wider.

"Can I taste you, baby?"

"Suck on my tits, please? They're so sensitive, Uncle Grant." Mina pleads with her gaze, her green eyes boring into mine. She lifts one heavy breast and offers it to me, her gaze dreamy as it slides across my face. She squeezes the engorged peak of her nipple, and creamy, white liquid dribbles out. I watch as it pools and then drips down her silken skin.

Mina drags her finger through the trail and brings it to my lips. I suck on the tip and taste the forbidden, salty, umami colostrum. My eyes roll back in my head as a low growl rumbles from deep in the back of my throat. When she squeezes, more dribbles from the pink tip, and I latch on in one smooth motion.

I suck and nibble on Mina's tits while she writhes and squirms beneath me. I feel her fingers drag through my hair, raking my scalp as I lap up every blessed drop of her juices. I slide a hand between us and push my fingers deep inside her. Mina cries out, her sharp nails digging into the nape of my neck.

I look up, her stiff tit still between my lips. Mina's eyes are shut, a look of utter ecstasy spread across her face.

"Don't stop, Uncle Grant."

Her breathless, needy words spur me on. I spit on her clit and rub it in with my thumb while I finger fuck her. Feeling her pussy juice drip down my wrist, I salivate at the hot, wet sound of her pleasure. Her legs flatten on the bed, and her back arches as she nears her climax. Her body tenses, her breath hitches in her throat, and she fists her hand in my hair. I suckle harder, flicking my tongue across the engorged bud, lapping up every precious dribble until she's calling out my name, core clenching around my fingers.

I disengage from her breast, panting and licking my lips. Her body convulses below me, and she lets out a low, steady moan.

"Ride the wave, princess. Chase that high all the way back to me," I coo, watching her body tense and release. Her fingers knot in the white sheets, and her legs tighten around my shoulders. Her ragged breath rattles in her heaving chest as I withdraw and slide down her body. I kiss her belly and her mound. I lap up her orgasm with one slick swipe of my tongue.

The sheets are soaked with colostrum and cum. The room

reeks of skin, sweat, and sex. My head swims with the scent of Mina's desire hanging heavy in the air. I watch as her eyes flutter open, and she takes a long, shuddering breath.

"How was that for a wedding night, Mrs. Wolf?" I chuckle, watching as Mina grabs a pillow and throws it at my head.

"Say it again," she whispers.

"Say what?"

"My last name."

I grin. "Mrs. Wolf."

Chapter Ten

The next four weeks fly by in a whirlwind. Mina and I pick out our wedding rings. We tell our friends, and we tell her father. Roger blows his top, as expected. He vows our friendship is over, and he wants nothing to do with either of us. Mina cries in my arms on the way home, and I've never seen her more upset in my life. She cries for days, and the only thing I can do is hold her and reassure her that I'll never be like that with our child.

The board finds my replacement, a young man with impeccable business sense. Handing over the reins goes smoothly and within a week, he's up and running the company. I quietly remove myself from daily operations, ready to let the young buck take over. I officially retire from my position as CEO and devote my time and energy toward setting up a home for Mina and our baby. The house we've been living in is massive, but it's just that: a house. It's not a home. It's not cozy. It's not warm with love. When I look at it, I don't see our child running through the halls. I don't see a future. And with that, we decide to move.

Mina finds us a home just before her twenty-week appointment, and I make the arrangements to have the old house packed, the new home set up, and the nursery painted. We argue back and forth over the color scheme, not knowing if we'll be having a boy or a girl, but, eventually, Mina wins. We have it painted a bright and cheery green, and Mina gets into decorating it. Right at twenty weeks, we settle into our new home, and our life as a married couple begins.

On Monday, we walk into the doctor's office hand in hand, ready to find out the sex of our baby. We faffed back and forth over finding out for days. I wanted to know, and she wanted to be surprised, then I wanted to be surprised, and she wanted to know. We spent hours poring over baby names online, staring at the sonogram photos, and trying to figure out by the way she carries whether it will be a boy or a girl. I reassure Mina that all I want is a healthy baby. Boy or girl, I'm committed to loving this child the way I love their mother.

The medical assistant takes us back to the exam room, and I feel my palms begin to shake and sweat. I've never been more jittery in my entire life. Mina takes my hand in hers, squeezing my fingers. She smiles at me and leans her head against me as I stand beside the exam table. The MA runs Mina's vitals, makes small talk, and I don't hear a word she says. I'm so focused on the life ahead of us that I don't even notice when the ultrasound tech comes in.

"Ready to see your baby?" she pipes up cheerfully, snapping me back to reality. Mina looks up at me, winks, and then turns back to the tech.

"We sure are. Ready, Daddy?"

I resist the urge to growl in my throat when she calls me Daddy. She's never called me that before. Even though she's calling me that in reference to our baby, it sparks a need inside me.

"Yes."

The tech shows us the screen and points out the important parts, like how the baby is measuring and how strong their heartbeat is. She points out the head, the toes, and their little fingers. She explains everything each step of the way, soothing my nerves. She and Mina make polite small talk as the tech runs her scans and then she says the words we've been waiting to hear.

"Ready to find out the sex?"

"Yes!" Mina and I chime in at the same time. We look at each other and then laugh. The tech smiles at us and places her ultrasound wand over Mina's belly, then tells us what we've been dying to know. Mina holds her breath and squeezes my fingers.

"You're having a girl. A very healthy-looking baby girl."

My wind knocks out of my lungs, and I feel as though I've been kicked in the gut. I blink back tears and beam at Mina as the realization washes over me.

A daughter. I'm going to have a daughter.

I lean down, kiss the top of Mina's head, and wipe away her tears. The ultrasound tech looks on in happiness and then tells Mina what's next. She prints the sonogram, labeled at the top with 'It's a girl!' When she hands us both a copy, I tuck mine into my wallet, right beside the first sonogram. My heart beats out of my chest and when the ultrasound tech leaves the room, giving us some privacy, I break down.

"You're gonna be a girl dad, Grant. Can you imagine?"

I can't form the words, and Mina strokes my cheek, tears welling up in her eyes. I pull her to me, wrapping my arms around her.

"I've had butterflies in my stomach for weeks, waiting to find out," I confide, choking on tears. Mina chuckles and grabs my hand, placing it over her belly.

"So have I."

I feel a fluttering. An actual, honest-to-God fluttering in her stomach. A lump forms in my throat when I realize what it is.

It's my daughter. It's our daughter.

Chapter Eleven

The entire walk out of the office and back to the car, my hand doesn't leave Mina's belly. I'm obsessed with feeling our daughter move within her, feeling her flutters. Mina laughs at me, but I don't care. I've never felt anything like it. I never knew I could feel anything like this.

On the drive home, Mina's hand doesn't leave mine. She squeezes my fingers and rubs my knuckles with her thumb. She brings our hands to her lips and kisses them, smiling at me.

"So, I suppose we should start thinking about names?" She broaches the subject carefully, as though trying to gauge my reaction. My heart flutters, and my eyes well up with tears. Baby names. What a thought.

"How about Caroline?"

"How about Marie?"

"How about Elizabeth?" The name trips off her tongue with ease, and I know that's the one. Elizabeth Wilhemina Wolf.

"That's it," I say softly. Mina looks at me with softness and smiles, her face splitting wide as she grins.

"Really? It was that easy?"

"It was that easy." I kiss her cheek and run my hand over her belly once we're in the driveway. Our daughter, our Elizabeth, flutters, and I know it's right. I know this is it. I lean close to Mina's belly and rub her roundness.

"Hi, Elizabeth. This is your dad. I…" I stop, choking back tears. I swallow the lump in my throat and continue while Mina rubs my shoulder and strokes the back of my neck. "This is your dad, baby girl. I can't wait to meet you. I can't wait to hold you and see your face. I can't wait to hold you. Don't be in too much of a rush to get here. Just know we're waiting for you."

A tear rolls down my cheek and lands on her blouse. I've never been so consumed with love in my life. I didn't know I could love like this before Mina came into my life. Now, that love has multiplied tenfold for our daughter. I never knew it could be like this. I never knew it could be this good.

"Take us inside, Daddy," Mina says softly. There it is again. Daddy.

"What did you call me?"

"Daddy?" She's shy about it; I can tell. It's one thing to call me 'Uncle Grant' in bed. To hear her call me 'Daddy' sparks an entirely new emotion in me. It sparks my desire, but it also makes my inner bear come out. I want to love her, I want to fuck her, and I want to protect her and our baby even more.

"Do you like that? It's not too much?"

"Princess, you can call me whatever you want. Daddy. Uncle Grant. Whatever you want."

"Take us inside, Uncle Grant. You can be Daddy to our daughter, but you'll always be Uncle Grant to me. Now, take us inside. I want to lie down."

"Can we lie down together?" I ask, kissing her belly one more time.

"I wouldn't have it any other way."

We make our way into our new home, passing the green nursery. I stop in the doorway and marvel at it, knowing that, soon, our daughter will be in there. It puts a lump in my throat, but I quickly push it away as Mina tugs me into the bedroom. She kicks her shoes off and removes her clothes, lying on the bed in her underwear.

I follow her lead and strip down to my boxers, joining her on top of the sheets. She rolls her body to face me, her belly between us. She's never looked more beautiful in all the days we've been together. She rubs her belly and looks up at me with her big, doe eyes.

"I never thought we'd be here," she says softly.

"What do you mean?"

"When I walked into your office last year, I never thought we'd be in bed together, growing a life between us. I thought…" She trails off and casts her eyes down.

"What did you think?"

"I thought it would be a one-time thing."

I cup her cheek, turning her face so her gaze meets mine. "It could never be a one-time thing between us. I fell in love with you the moment you walked through my door, before I even knew it was you. You stole my heart with a look, and I knew once I had you in my bed, I could never let you go."

"Did you always plan on marrying me?"

"You stole my heart and turned my world upside down. I reconsidered my entire life when you walked in. And when you told me you were pregnant? I knew I needed to make you my wife. I needed to make you my everything, my only thing, forever."

"Are you sad we didn't go to a courthouse and do it legally?"

I shake my head. "No. I don't need a piece of paper to make you my wife. I don't need a piece of paper to show the world how much I love you, Mina. I am yours, and you are mine."

"What about our daughter?"

I kiss her forehead and whisper, "She is ours. Nothing will ever change that."

Mina looks up at me, and I see something lighting her eyes from within. It's not the desire I'm used to seeing. It's not sharp, intense passion. It's softer, rounder, deeper. She places her hand on my chest and tangles her fingers in the fine, downy hair.

"I love you."

"I know."

"I've loved you my entire life, Uncle Grant. Since I was a girl. I dreamed of being your wife when I was little. And now, here

I am. Here we are."

"Here we are. Married. In love. About to be parents to our daughter."

"Would you change anything?"

"No. Not a damn thing. Would you?"

"Not a single thing."

She runs her fingers up my chest to my cheek and brings our lips together. It's the sweetest kiss I've ever tasted. I melt against her mouth, and my hands begin to explore her curves. I rub her belly, trace the slope of her hips, and palm her breasts until she's mewling beneath my touch.

She breaks the chain of kisses I leave along her cheek and jaw, her voice soft.

"I need you."

"I need you too, baby girl."

"No. I need you. I need to feel you inside me. Now."

"Now?"

"Now. Fuck me, Uncle Grant. Please?"

"You don't ever have to beg me, baby girl. But I'll do you one better. I'll make love to you."

"That is better. Make love to me."

"Of course, princess."

Chapter Twelve

When I look at Mina now, naked in my arms, I don't see the sex kitten who strolled into my office and stole my heart. I don't see the little girl I knew all those years ago. I see a grown woman. I see the mother of my child. I see my wife. I see the way her body has changed in the last year. The way she's softened, the way she's rounded out, the way she's blossomed. I take all that into consideration when we make love.

I roll her onto her side and ease her into position, placing a pillow under her belly. She pulls her panties down, and I unhook her bra, slowly removing them and dropping them on the floor in a pile with my boxers. She pulls me close, grabbing my arm and wrapping it around her as I position myself. She lifts her leg and turns to grant me better access to her honey pot. When I slip inside, we both sigh with relief. I slide my fingers down her belly to her mound and begin to play her like a fiddle.

She's so wet for me, my cock slides in and out easily, even in this position. The sound of skin on skin fills the air between her moans and my groans of pleasure. She calls me love names and entwines our fingers as they rest on her belly. The entire time I'm inside her, I feel the fluttering in her womb. I feel her body tense around me as her cunt contracts, milking my dick with each stroke. She whimpers when I slide out and kiss her neck as I reposition myself.

"Don't stop, Grant," she breathes, whining while I roll her back onto her side.

"Easy, princess. I'm just readjusting," I coo. I push her bent knee toward her belly and slide onto my knees, pushing my cock inside her. A low groan escapes my lips as I sink into her wetness, and she arches her back in pleasure.

I thrust slowly, letting her acclimate to my rhythm. She reaches for my hand, and we lock fingers again as I lean over her. I kiss her shoulder and pick up my pace. Her pussy welcomes every inch of me like a glove, contracting and clenching while she thumbs her clit. I love watching her play with herself. I love watching her pleasure build from the inside out. She palms the outside of her pussy, working her fingers in tight circles while I slam into her.

"Are you close baby girl?" I ask, already knowing the answer. I know her body, and I know the sounds she makes when she wants to release everything she's been holding back. Her little whimpers, her deep moans, the cute way she says, 'Fuck, Uncle Grant, harder!' It drives me wild and pushes me closer to my own release.

"Mhm," she moans, biting her lip. I reach up and stroke her hair, gripping it at the base of her neck the way I know she enjoys. I tense my fingers and rake my nails against her scalp, and she purrs like a kitten.

"Come for me, princess. Come all over your favorite uncle's cock," I whisper in her ear. Her entire body convulses, and she cries out as her pleasure crests. My name has never sounded as sweet as it does when it comes from her lips. The way she moans for me, the way she whimpers, it sets my hips rocking faster and faster while the pleasure builds in the base of my spine.

She comes, her body releasing all the tension in her muscles, and she exhales the breath she's been holding in. I follow close behind, tipping over the edge into an orgasm that rocks my entire body. I shoot my load inside her, my fingers digging into the meat of her thigh as I release. I shut my eyes and lean over her, putting my lips to her cheek. Once I'm spent, I roll over onto my back, panting like a beast in heat.

Mina rolls her body into me, and my arms wrap around her instinctively. We lie together, breathless and calm, for a long time, soaking in each other's afterglow. I stroke the length of her spine and kiss her head as I recover, whispering love words into her ear. She nuzzles closer to me, our legs tangling together under the duvet we've kicked down the bed.

After a few quiet moments, Mina's sleepy voice comes out, and she whispers, "I love you, Grant."

"I love you too, Mina." I wrap my arm tighter around her shoulders, my other hand resting comfortably on her belly.

"Let's make it official."

"Make what official, baby girl?"

"Our marriage. Let's go to the courthouse. Let's go out in the woods with a justice of the peace. Let's go to Vegas. I don't care how we do it."

"Why, baby? I thought we didn't need a piece of paper to show our commitment to each other."

She looks up at me with her big doe eyes, and I feel my heart melt. No matter what she says next, I know I'm going to give her what she wants.

"I want our daughter to grow up in a home where she knows her parents love each other. I want what my parents—flawed as they were—I want what they had. Please, Grant? Please, can we get married for real?"

"Of course, princess. If you want the whole nine yards, the house with the white picket fence, the dog in the yard, two-and-a-half kids—" She cuts me off with a giggle.

"Let's just have this one first. And our house already has a white fence. Please?"

I kiss the tip of her nose and trail my finger down her cheek. Her eyes lock on mine, and she pouts. It takes all I have not to burst into laughter at the sight. I'm not even going to make her work for it. I'm going to give Mina exactly what she wants.

"Of course, we can get married, baby. You pick a day, a time, and a dress code, and I'll be there with bells on. If you want to get married tomorrow, we'll go get the license in the morning. If you want to wait, I'll wait as long as it takes. You're already my wife in my heart. What's another day?"

Mina's tiny hand snakes up my chest and cups my cheek as she kisses me. Her cheeks are pink and radiating heat, and I've never felt such happiness in her kiss before. She kisses me deeply and then pulls away breathlessly.

"Let's do it. Tomorrow. Take me to the courthouse, Uncle Grant, and let's make it official."

"Anything you want, baby girl. But for now?"

"For now?"

"Let's take a nap. I'm exhausted." I yawn. The adrenaline from our love-making session has worn off, and now I'm fighting off the sleep that threatens to claim me.

"Of course. Oh, and Uncle Grant?"

"Yes, princess?"

"I love you."

"I know you do. Come here."

I wrap my arms around her as she snuggles into my chest. She absently strokes my thigh with the tip of her finger until she falls asleep, and I soon tumble after her into dreamland.

Tomorrow, she'll be my wife, and not just in name only. We'll join our lives together legally, and our daughter will grow up in a home with a mother and father who love each other and would do anything for her. She'll grow up knowing her daddy loves her mommy more than life itself, and she'll grow up knowing that everything I've done, I've done for them.

I dream of Mina in a white dress.

Chapter Thirteen

In the morning, Mina and I get dressed separately, taking turns in the closet. I opt for a suit coat and khakis, trying to keep it casual. The butterflies in my stomach threaten to spill out with each breath as I wait for her in the living room. We're only going to the courthouse, I remind myself every few minutes. I stare at the clock on the wall, at the screen of my phone, and out the window while I try to calm my nerves.

At eleven, Mina comes down the stairs, and my jaw hits the floor. She looks like a vision in the morning light as she comes into the living room, a form-hugging white dress wrapped around her curves. Her red hair frames her face in carefully coiffed waves, and her green eyes shine bright under dark, heavy lashes. She looks absolutely stunning as she makes her way to me, and I stumble to my feet. I wrap my arms around her and inhale the familiar floral perfume she wears just for me.

"How do I look?"

I run my hand over my jaw and fumble for words. "Baby girl, you look—I've never seen you so—You're beautiful. You're so beautiful."

She smiles demurely and plants a kiss on my cheek. "Are you ready to do this?"

"Baby, I'm as ready as I'll ever be."

Mina grabs my hand and places it over her belly. I feel the fluttering of our daughter beneath my palm, and I beam at Mina. I rub my hand across the meridian of her belly and lean down, placing a kiss on top. My lips linger a moment.

"Hi, sweet girl. This is your daddy."

The fluttering continues, and I smile. I lay my head against Mina, and she strokes my hair while I whisper to our girl.

"I'm going to marry your mommy today. You're gonna grow up in a house where your parents love each other more than life itself, and we'll do anything for you. I didn't know love until your mommy came into my life, and now I have more than my fair share of it. We can't wait to meet you, Elizabeth. Don't be in too much of a hurry to get here."

Mina strokes the back of my neck and shoulders while I leave one last kiss for our daughter. She tugs me up by the scruff of my neck and looks at me, her eyes dark with desire. Mina licks her lips and leans in, kissing me with passion and fire. I wrap my arms around her and hold her tight, my grip steady as she rocks into me.

When she breaks away, breathless, I stare at her curiously. I'm not complaining about her sudden rush of lust, but I do have questions.

"What was that about, baby girl?"

She looks up at me and shrugs, a sly smile tugging up the corner of her perfect pout. "There's something inexplicably sexy about you talking to our daughter."

"Are you saying I should talk to her more often? Because if you're going to kiss me like that every time? I'll talk to her night and day." I laugh, brushing a strand of hair from her eyes.

"You should talk to her every day. I do."

"You do?"

"The first things a baby hears are their mother's heartbeat and then her voice. I want her to know me before she even meets me. I want her to know her daddy, too." She takes my hand in hers and brings it to her lips. "I want her to know you before she's born."

A tear comes to my eye, and I try to blink it away. I've never thought of it that way. Our daughter can hear us. She knows who we are. I should be talking to her every night. I should be reading her stories. I should be… My thoughts spiral, and I feel an immense pang of guilt. There's so much more I should be doing, but I don't know where to start.

"Come on. We've got a reservation to keep." Mina laughs, stirring me from my thoughts. I shake my head to clear it and beam at her, intertwining my fingers in hers.

"Baby girl, you know you don't make reservations at the courthouse."

"No, but you do have to make them at Veronica's for lunch. And if we want to make it by one, we've got to get going."

My heart jumps into my throat. Veronica's. The restaurant where it all began. Mina thought of everything.

We make our way to the car, and I let Felix, our driver, take the wheel. Mina and I slide into the back seat, and she leans her head against my shoulder as we pull out of the driveway and onto the open road. Our fingers locked together, I kiss the top of her head. Felix looks back at us in the rearview mirror and winks, tapping the button for the partition.

"That won't be necessary, Felix," I say, shaking my head.

"Yeah, but that lovey-dovey shit is catching." He laughs. I grin at him and nod, letting him put up the wall for a few minutes to give Mina and me total privacy. We make the drive in comfortable silence, fingers locked, head on shoulder, hand on belly. Neither of us says a word, and we don't have to. Everything is comfortable between us.

"Grant?" Mina pipes up in a small voice as we pull into the courthouse parking garage.

"Yes, sweetheart?"

"I love you."

"I know you do, baby girl. I love you, too."

"Thank you."

"For what?"

"For everything you've given me."

"Mina, if that's the case, I should be thanking you."

"What do you mean?"

OLIVE SPENCER

I don't have a chance to answer before Felix pulls alongside the entrance to the courthouse and steps out to open the door. I slide out, offer Mina my hand, and assist her out of the car. She wobbles slightly in kitten heels, and her dress has slid up her thighs. I distract Felix while she adjusts herself and when she's ready, Mina slides her hand into the crook of my elbow.

"Thank you, Felix."

"No problem, boss. I'll wait here."

"Good man." He tips his cap to me and slides back into the driver's seat. I take Mina's hand, and we walk into the courthouse together.

The clerk at the desk welcomes us, eyeing us with curiosity. Mina tells the young man what we're here to do, and he pulls out a stack of paperwork for us to fill out, directing us to sit in the lobby. We do as we're told and take our seats. I take on the task of the mountain of paperwork while Mina fixes her makeup in a compact.

"What did you mean, in the car?"

"When?"

"When you said you should be thanking me."

I set the paperwork on the table beside us and turn in the seat. I cup Mina's face in my palm and stroke her cheek while I speak.

"Baby girl, you've given me everything. Everything I ever needed. You made our house a home. You're carrying our child. You're giving me your hand, from now until forever. You are my everything, Mina Maguire."

She giggles and replies, "Don't you mean Mina Wolf?"

I chuckle. "Of course. You are my everything, Mina Wolf. You and our daughter are my entire world." I squeeze her fingers and resume filling out the paperwork. I walk it over to the clerk and hand it to him with a smile while he looks it over.

"You forgot one question, sir. Are you two blood relatives, or otherwise related?"

I laugh and shake my head as he hands the paperwork back across the desk. "No, son. No blood relation between her and

I." I cross off the box and slide it back for his perusal one more time.

"Perfect. This is all in order. The justice will see you now."

I walk back to Mina with a grin as wide as a country mile on my face and assist her to her feet.

"This is it, princess. Are you ready?"

"Ready as I'll ever be," she teases, sticking her tongue out at me. I roll my eyes and shake my head.

"I'm never going to live that down, am I?"

"Not on your life. Now, lead the way."

I take Mina by the hand and lead her into the courtroom, where a justice of the peace awaits, along with two witnesses.

I take the deepest breath of my life, and the justice begins his spiel.

Chapter Fourteen

The ceremony is short and sweet. The justice of the peace keeps it light, makes a few jokes, and keeps us on our toes. At the end, Mina and I sign our marriage license, and it's official. We're husband and wife. Not just playing house, not pretending, actually husband and wife. It hits me all at once. A wave of emotions courses through me, making me giddy. I've never felt like this before, not even with my ex-wife. I've never known a love like this all-consuming love. Mina, my everything, my lawfully wedded wife. Grant and Mina Wolf. Husband, wife, and a baby on the way.

Felix greets us cheerfully as we exit the courthouse, popping a confetti streamer as we reach the car. Mina giggles, and I shake his hand, a wide grin lighting up my face. He congratulates us warmly and asks where we want to go next. Mina instructs him to drive us to Veronica's, and we slide into the back seat, all laughter and cheer.

"Partition, boss? Missus boss?"

Mina looks at me with mischief in her eye. "Roll it up please, Felix. My husband and I need to have a little chat."

Felix winks at me in the rearview, and the partition rolls up slowly. He pulls out of the parking garage and onto the street, pointing the car toward the restaurant.

"So, you wanted to have a 'little chat'?" I turn to Mina,

raising my eyebrow and fighting back a chuckle.

"I wanted you all to myself for a few minutes. I wanted my husband all to myself." She leans over and kisses my cheek, her lips lingering a moment. I feel her long false lashes tickle my cheek, and I shut my eyes, relishing in the moment alone.

"And what did you want me all to yourself for, Mrs. Wolf?" I murmur into her ear as she nuzzles my neck. She settles against me, her head on my shoulder and her hand on my thigh.

"Did you ever think it would be like this, Mr. Wolf? Did you ever imagine we would be this happy?"

I wrap my arm around her, resting my palm on her belly. My fingers trace along the curve, and I close my eyes, inhaling her soft, comforting scent.

"Before you, Mina? I never thought I'd be happy again. I was married to Wolf Industries. I was a man with nothing in his life but work. I was too busy working to live. But when you walked into my office last summer in that too-tight skirt?"

"It wasn't that tight!" She giggles, and the sound warms me through like a shot of whiskey. I squeeze her and kiss her forehead before continuing.

"When you waltzed into my office, proclaiming your 'grown woman needs'? You breathed new life into these old bones. You gave me everything my life was missing. You brought me joy. You brought me love. You painted my life in vivid technicolor. I did not know I would be this happy, but I do know this. I wouldn't change it for the world."

She traces her finger in circles on my thigh and sighs with contentment. "I never thought I could be this happy either."

"That's all I get? I spill my soul to you, and that's all I get?" I shake with laughter, and Mina's soft giggle fills the space between us.

"What else would you have me say that I haven't already said?"

"Tell me you love me without saying you love me."

"That's easy. I can do that in two words."

"Oh, and how's that?"

"All I have to do… is call you Uncle Grant." She looks up at me and bats her lashes, and I feel warm all over. Heat spreads through my chest and tingles in my limbs as she stares into my soul with her big, doe eyes.

"Touché, Mrs. Wolf."

I cup her chin and bring our lips together as we pull into the parking lot of Veronica's. Felix rolls up alongside the building and steps out, rushing around to open the door for us. I slide out, offering Mina my hand before pressing a crisp one-hundred-dollar bill into Felix's palm.

Veronica herself greets us at the door. She looks at me, then Mina, and a soft, warm smile spreads across her face.

"Grant! It's so good to see you again. It's been quite some time, from the looks of it." She winks at Mina, and my wife blushes, her fingers intertwining with mine.

"Too long, Veronica. Too long. Mina and I are celebrating today, and where else should we celebrate but where it all began for us?"

"Perfect. We do love a celebration. I've reserved your table in the back, if you'll follow me." She grabs two menus and leads us through the restaurant. For lunchtime, it's quiet, and there are few other patrons in the dining room. She ushers us to the table and holds out Mina's chair. Veronica lays the menus on the table and excuses herself, assuring us that our waiter will be with us shortly.

I don't even look at the menu, I'm so busy staring at my wife. Wife, wife, wife. The word echoes in my head like the refrain of an old, familiar song, spreading warmth throughout my body. I reach across the table and take Mina's hand in mine, smiling at her as she looks up from the menu. In the afternoon light, she's never looked so radiant. She's never glowed like this. She's lit up from the inside, and it makes me feel gooey. It make me feel young.

"What's that for? That look on your face?" She eyes me curiously, a gentle smile tugging up the corner of her mouth.

"I love you, Mina. I love you so much. You've never looked so beautiful, and I don't ever want this day to end."

She melts, squeezing my fingers. "I love you too, Grant. This day never has to end, you know. I'm yours, for the rest of our lives. We can live this day over and over again."

"You only have one wedding day, baby girl," I remind her with a chuckle.

"Well, in your case, you only have three."

OLIVE SPENCER

Epilogue

Twenty weeks become ten, become five, become two. Before I know it, I'm packing go bags and leaving them by the door, just in case. I spend every hour of every day tending to Mina and her every need. I rub cocoa and shea butter into her belly and massage her back before bed. I braid her hair when she gets too hot and too restless to sleep. I read books to our daughter in the womb until Mina is the one falling asleep, her head lolling against my shoulder. I spend every waking moment I can preparing for the next phase of our lives.

I wrap up my business for the month early, close down my consulting hours, and set my out-of-office email for the week Mina is due. We count down the hours, waiting every day for the contractions to start. By Thursday night, there's still no change. Mina, round with our child, is miserable and ready to pop. She tries everything to induce labor. Spicy foods. Long walks. Gentle exercise. More spicy foods. On Friday morning, Mina is practically in tears waiting for her water to break. It makes my heart ache to see her so downtrodden and uncomfortable, and I find myself searching the internet for ways to speed up the process.

The web is full of ideas, but one sticks out to me in particular. Sex. The old wives of the web claim having sex will induce labor naturally. When I suggest it to Mina, she looks at me like I'm crazy.

"I'm the size of a house, Grant," she protests, rubbing her lower back while she paces the living room floor. Her belly sticks out like she swallowed a watermelon, and I can see how much discomfort she's in from the way she rocks back and forth when she stops. She shifts from foot to foot, rolls her head shoulder to shoulder, and releases a sigh from deep inside.

"What if it helps, baby?" I slide behind her, guiding her to the couch. She eases into a sitting position and leans against the back of the couch, eyes shut.

"But... I'm so gross. I'm fat, I haven't shaved in months, I can't see my—"

"Princess, I don't care. I want to help you feel better. I want to make you comfortable."

She rolls her head to the side, cocks one eye open, and considers me carefully. Mina chews her lip while she weighs her options, and I stifle a chuckle.

"What's so funny?"

"Did you ever think you'd have to decide whether you wanted to have sex with me or not?"

A peal of laughter escapes her pretty pink lips, and it makes my heart pound. "No, I suppose I never have. I've always wanted to have sex with you, Grant."

"And what about now?"

"Are you sure... Are you sure it'll help?"

"Would the women of the internet lie?"

Mina laughs again, her belly shaking. "Fine, fine. Fuck me. I want this baby out. Now."

"Always the romantic, Mina." I laugh, sliding closer to her on the couch. She turns to face me and puts my hand on her knee, pushing it under her skirt.

"If we're going to fuck this baby out, we better get started."

"Slowly, baby girl. It's too good of a job to rush."

I slide my hand under her skirt, caressing her thigh and sliding my palm up the length of her leg. I feel the heat radiating from the apex of her thighs and the urgency of her kiss as she grinds against my palm. Her panties are soaked and as I work my hand under the waistband, she stops kissing me. Mina pulls back with a look of shock on her face, looks down at the couch, then stares at me, mouth agape.

"What's wrong? What is it?" My voice rises with concern, and I stare at her, trying to understand why she stopped so suddenly.

"Uncle Grant? I think my water just broke." Her voice is small. Her eyes are wide. I can feel her heartbeat from across the couch, and I know this is it. The baby is coming.

"Oh, shit. Oh, shit. Oh, shit!"

I don't have time to think before I'm grabbing her go bag and rushing her into the car. I call the hospital from the road, trying to keep my voice calm while a flood of emotions rushes through me. Mina squeezes my fingers the entire way, clenching and unclenching as contractions come and go. By the time we reach the hospital, I'm sure my hand is bruised beyond recognition, but I don't care. I'm going to be a dad. I'm going to be a father.

We're taken to labor and delivery and shown into a room. Mina changes into a hospital gown, and I reassure her she's never looked more radiant. An epidural is given, and Mina cries like I've never seen. I kiss away her tears, cooing in her ear about her strength and what a wonderful mother she's going to make. I tell her all the plans we're going to make for our daughter's future. I hold her hand, rub her back, and push her hair out of her face. Not once does Mina tell me to leave, and not once does she say she hates me. We hang onto each other for dear life while we wait to welcome this new life into the world.

The hours tick by, and the contractions come closer and closer. The doctor comes in and tells us it's finally time. Mina pushes, and pushes, and pushes. It feels like hours and then suddenly, our daughter is here. She lets out one little chirp of a cry, and I feel my heart shatter into a million tiny pieces. Mina and I look at each other while they clean our daughter, and the tears begin to fall freely. When they put our daughter on Mina's chest and I see her look into her mother's face, I completely break down. I've never been so happy in my entire life.

When I'm allowed to hold her, Elizabeth Wilhelmina Wolf, all seven pounds, nine ounces, and twenty tiny inches fits along the length of my forearm. Mina hands her to me after nursing, and I marvel at our daughter. She's so pink and new; I'm afraid of breaking her. She has her mother's green eyes and the tiniest wisps of copper hair atop her head. It fills my heart with joy to see how much like Mina she looks, and I'm struck with sentiment.

"Hi, Little Red," I whisper. She stirs and whimpers, snuggling into my arms and quieting after a few moments. We sink into the rocking chair beside the bed where Mina rests, dozing peacefully. I rock my daughter to sleep, humming to her while her mother dreams beside us. I never thought I would have this life. I thought I was destined to be the cold businessman my father was, the cold businessman his father was before him. All that changed the moment Mina Maguire walked into my office, demanded a summer job, and stole my heart.

Mina wakes sometime later and spies me singing to our daughter. Her hand snakes out across the bed and finds mine, our fingers entwining. Neither of us says a word, and we don't need to. We sit in the comfortable quiet and stare at the beautiful baby we made, the new love of our lives. Mina and I take turns holding Elizabeth and when it's Mina's turn, I slip out to bring her snacks and ice chips.

I return, stopping in the doorway. Mina sings to Elizabeth, rocking her in her arms, and I realize this is my life now. This is our life now.

Mina was everything I wasn't supposed to want. But Mina and Elizabeth? They're everything I've ever wanted and more.

THE END

OLIVE SPENCER

Acknowledgements

As always, I want to thank my friends in a specific Discord server for encouraging me to write. This wouldn't have happened without your constant poking.

I am eternally grateful to the makers of Diet Coke, for without their nectar of the gods, I would not have had been able to focus long enough to get Grant and Mina's story on the page.

I owe a large debt to the creators of Youtube, my friends on Twitter, and the few people in real life who know who Olive Spencer is.

Thank you, each and every one of you.

Oh, and a special thank you to Hannah Green for editing this series. Grant and Mina owe you their lives.

About the Author

Olive Spencer is a renowned author known for her steamy, one-handed reads that leave readers sweating, panting, and begging for more. Her works feature a blend of contemporary and paranormal erotic romance with a focus on handsome vampires, sexy older men, and powerful women who command every scene. Olive's books are packed with spice, offering sensual ménage à trois scenes, captivating ghost stories, and slightly forbidden romances that draw readers in and leave them with a book hangover rivaling that of cheap whiskey.

Beyond her writing, Olive's personal life is just as intriguing. When she isn't crafting her next spicy tale behind her trusty MacBook, Olive enjoys relaxing with a Diet Coke while indulging in soap operas or exploring local bookstores. Often found with headphones on, she's likely listening to a spicy audiobook or her favorite country song, 'Dicked Down in Dallas'. Olive may not be a Gemini vegetarian, but she is a fan of Reese Witherspoon movies and knows every line from the greatest rom-com ever made, 'Sweet Home Alabama.'

For more about Olive Spencer and her tantalizing tales, visit her website: olivespencer.com

Where to find Olive Online

Olive Spencer is (still) on Twitter. Join her at @misskmagpie.
She's on Threads and Instagram @ospencersmut.
She's on Bluesky as @misskmagpie.bsky.social
You can find her on Facebook as Olive Spencer - Author

If you want to visit her website, you can find Olive online at www.olivespencer.com and her books are available at www.library.olivespencer.com

Thank You

If you've read this far, you deserve a cookie, a glass of warm milk, and a blanket. Thank you so much.

Grant and Mina's story has come to an end, but there are plenty of other stories to be told. Stick around; you never know what you'll find.